Dancing on HOT Sand

How He Stole Her Man

By

E. McLeod Baines

About The Author

E. "McLeod" Baines was raised in the inner-city housing projects of Chicago. As a prodigy of the inner-city housing projects, it was constantly and irresponsibly repeated to him, as with numerous youth, teachers, friends and some family, that the housing projects would be his destiny. And if his mother were ever to relocate from the projects, the "project mentality" would remain.

They would say, "You can take the person from the projects, but the projects can never be taken from the person."

Internally, such careless and thoughtless pessimistic statements as this can penetrate and resonate deep within, thereby causing residual negative affects to numerous young lives.

The cascading effect of those defeatist attitudes, in many cases, may unfortunately cause the aspiring budding youth to fail, leaving nothing more than vain notions of emptiness toward a successful future.

E. McLeod Baines, driven with an abundance of self-determination, coupled with the support of his divorced parents, some close family members and a few outside influences, refused to succumb to the wiles of his surroundings.

He was the second in his family to graduate college, earning a B.A. with a double major in Business Administration and Spanish. His Uncle John a/k/a "Uncle Buddy", his mother's oldest brother, was the first.

While working full-time and simultaneously touring the country with the famed Thompson Community Singers, a gospel recording choir and the Joseph Holmes Dance Theater, he refused to allow the "Naysayers" to restrain his numerous aspirations.

He worked his way up the corporate ladder and ultimately became an award winning respected banking officer.

He continued to develop his many passions for American Sign Language, acting, playwright and piano skills.

Among numerous awards, he is the recipient of the prestigious **Dr. Martin Luther King Jr, Service Award** for his contribution to drama/theater for the development of programs and projects, which demonstrated concern for social issues.

Kindle Direct Printing
ISBN – 9781730958670

I dedicate this book to my family and friends who have demonstrated unlimited support throughout the years.

This book is a work of fiction

All content is purely a product of the author's creativity and imagination. Any resemblances of persons and/or events are strictly coincidental.

An Allegory

Visiting a beach on a moderately summer day can be intriguing. A walk on the beach in a hot climate can prove to be strangely exhilarating as you inhale the fresh air emanating from the water's gentle breeze.

But when your sandals are removed in order to feel the warmth of the sand between your toes, you instinctively either put your sandals back on or begin to jump, alternating your feet to prevent scorching until you become accustomed to the new sensation.

CHAPTER 1

Being somewhat of an introvert, I always secretly wanted someone to love and who would accept me for who I was. Being very light skinned, I was always told that I was either too light and my facial features of curly light brown hair and light hazel brown eyes were not *black enough.*

I was often told by peers that I was too light for a girlfriend of color and too dark to be called or accepted by whites. With the exception of relatives and a few close friends, half-breed was a name I was cruelly called.

Often being mistaken for mixed or Puerto Rican, was for some strange reason taboo in my poverty stricken, all black neighborhood, as well as in numerous areas in which I travelled.

I recall a girl whom I befriended telling me that she thought I was cute, which naturally made me feel good. I then returned the compliment.

But then she said "Jabarai, if you ever want to have sex, we can do it, but you're too *high yellow* for me to accept you as a boyfriend.

I like my men chocolate." Needless to say, I was insulted at the cruelty of her thoughtless, insensitive and unsolicited advance and callous statement and immediately terminated our "so-called" friendship.

Yes, she was attractive and I possibly could have eventually seen her as a potential *love bug*.

Unlike many other guys my age who would have jumped at the opportunity to simply "hit it and quit it", I typically viewed life somewhat differently, thus causing a waning desire for a closer relationship.

I assume her hurtful words resonated subliminally deep within, thus causing me to become somewhat withdrawn from attempting to have a girlfriend.

I then began to focus more on various school activities. Bonding with a few individuals, mostly male, inside and outside of my neighborhood who seemingly weren't color-struck or insensitive to complexion differences became my primary focus.

The racial diversity of the school setting seemed to be where I apparently most comfortably fit in.

I eventually saw a white girl by the name of Nancy in one of my classes who seemed to be quite nice and attractive. On a scale of 1 to 10, I gave her a 7 or 8.

After long deliberation, I decided to ask her out on a date. I suggested that possibly we could do lunch or go somewhere after school for a snack.

She politely but nervously stated that although she thought I was nice, she didn't date black guys. It never occurred to me that her parents wouldn't allow her to do so, even if she wanted to.

After disappointment number two, I again became withdrawn and retreated to my secret closet of disappointment and despair.

A while later during one of my classes I looked over and saw this pretty girl with flawless brown skin. She had long thick black hair and a petite cola shaped figure that any guy would love to date. She was the "icing on the cake," as the saying goes.

She was the semblance of a modern day Aphrodite-A goddess of beauty in every sense.

I thought she was so stunningly pretty and breathtaking that she simply had to have a boyfriend.

Although I didn't know her name, I, for some strange reason, just couldn't keep my eyes off of her. Concentration during class became extremely difficult.

Thoughts of her continually ran through my mind, but because she was so strikingly beautiful I thought I probably would be quickly rejected. I also thought she might have a color complex, like others I had encountered or overheard talking who were only seeking their *Chocolate Thunder Mandingo* dream man.

I often reflected on others who only wanted to be friends or secretly desired me as a *side-piece* solely because of my almost white complexion.

She always seemed so poised and polished that I discerned that she had to have more couth than others I had observed.

Unbeknownst to her I usually found ways to observe this goddess as she exited the class and school building. Like me, she typically engaged very few, if any, in idle conversation.

One day after class, I got up the nerve and with a bit of tension managed to strike up a dialogue. I had to ask her for her name and if she needed any help with class assignments.

In a beautiful high-pitched voice she told me her name was Lisa. I thought to myself finally I may be making some headway.

But then I must have gone a bit too far when I asked if I could walk her home.

"Thanks but, No thanks. Maybe some other time" She sweetly responded. Surely she must have known I had an interest in her. At least this wasn't an outright rejection and I felt I might have a chance.

Subconsciously her voice continued to be so memorizing, as if it could melt frozen butter with a cold knife. I couldn't stop thinking about her.

Each time in class, I found it hard to concentrate as I thought about her. I somehow couldn't keep my eyes off my new heartthrob.

Being persistent, I managed to befriend her by occasionally catching her eye and making my presence known via friendly smiles, followed by a sincere hellos and idle dialogue.

I always made sure I was in class early enough to start small conversations in order to help build trust. I apparently was finally making progress as she wasn't brushing me off, which she could have easily done.

Finally after her trust for me developed she allowed me walk her home, but would not let me in. She said she lived with her aunt and was not allowed to have company.

The more she resisted my advances to come in made the challenge all the more interesting. I knew then she had to have morals and didn't get passed around like many of the other girls I had so often heard about.

The thought of my light complexion standing out in a neighborhood where almost everyone was dark and the potential dangers of being identified in an area being jumped and robbed never crossed my mind.

Somehow the dangers of occasionally walking through neighborhoods where I seldom, if ever, saw someone of my light complexion began to sink in as others passed saying "Wassup Red?" Or "Aren't you too white to be in our neighborhood?"

To myself I always thought "I'm black too, but with less melanin." Obviously others didn't see it that way.

I often thought "Why are we as people of color so *color struck* or so rude about complexion differences? I simply wasn't raised that way."

Mama often reminded me that this was just the way of the world and racism exists on both sides of the track and often within our own culture.

In addition to blatant racism within my own culture, frightening thoughts began to resonate within me referencing the numerous hazards and dangers occurring in most neighborhoods. Even in my own taking public transportation, particularly at night through certain districts was known to be challenging.

Although I had no fear of the streets, I knew I had to look for other ways to safely get around.

I eventually convinced dad, who didn't live with me and mom, to co-sign for me to get a car. I promised to pay for it with my part-job.

He made me vow to stay in school if he assisted me. Being a young man of my word and integrity, he knew I was good for my promise.

But first I had to learn how to drive!

Here I was 19 and never been behind the wheel of a car. Mom, for some unexplained reason, didn't want me to drive. I think it was because a few years prior she almost lost her life in an accident.

Without mom's knowledge, I first got my learner's permit and with my savings I hired a driving instructor. I arranged for the instructor to provide the lessons while mom was at work.

After taking a few lessons I paid the instructor to take me to a facility where I could take the tests, both written and road. He picked me up in his personal car which was much larger than the one I was accustomed to that the driver's school provided.

I passed the written test receiving a score of 100%. What an awesome feeling it was to have received a perfect score. I thought after that I would immediately receive my license.

All I could think about was Lisa and how impressed she would be of me. How I surely wanted to impress her.

But then I was told to go to next line. It was time to take the road test. During my excitement I had either forgotten that an on-site road test along government property would be required or it was never fully explained.

My guess was when I heard of the perfect written test score I had received I would somehow be exempt from the road test since I had completed an *on the road* driver's education course.

On taking the required on the road test, the 3 point turn and other required maneuvers presented no problem. But then I was asked to parallel park, which I had only done once or twice, and that was in open and unrestricted space.

Needless to say, in my nervousness, I suddenly began to sweat profusely and horribly failed that part by knocking the flags over that served as make-shift cars.

I made the Department of Motor Vehicle man so nervous by knocking the flags down that he said although he shouldn't pass me, he graciously would. Then he sternly stated that he never wanted to see me there again.

I immediately received my temporary driver's license and was told the permanent license would be mailed within thirty days.

I was definitely on pins and needles at the thought of receiving my permanent license. Thoughts kept running through my head about what if the guy from the DMV changed his mind because of my parking blunder? If so, I would have to retake the road test. Who would I get to go with me and allow me to use their car?

The daily anticipation of waiting for the postman to deliver my permanent license was extremely nerve wrecking.

After about a week of nervous expectation, our friendly postman finally delivered my *special letter*. My license finally arrived. Upon receiving my permanent license, I immediately called dad and gave him the good news.

Within two weeks dad and I went car shopping. He kept his word, as I knew he would.

Soon afterwards, during one cold December evening, rather than fearlessly walking my new *friend* home, I decided to surprise Lisa about the news of my good fortune. Now in lieu of walking several blocks to her home, I could now proudly drive her home.

At first she was reluctant, but due to our increased level of friendship and trust that had developed between us, she finally gave in.

As the saying goes, I was in heaven.

CHAPTER 2

The short journey to where she resided was quite pleasant. I made sure I drove carefully and slowly. I didn't want our time together to end. Nor did I want her to know that I had just received my license and that I also had just learned how to drive.

Was I falling in love for the first time?

Since I had so often been rejected on many levels with others, platonic or otherwise usually because of my, as I was told, "high yellow" complexion, I had deep-seated reasons to doubt this relationship would go further. Nonetheless, I thought I would give it a try.

Upon reaching her residence I attempted a first kiss, but was quickly rejected with her placing her hand between us.

Since I was a virgin in all respects and had never been romantically kissed, I was ok with this rejection. As the saying goes, "You will never miss what you never had".

I assumed she was (1) following taught etiquette and strict protocol or (2) was not attracted to me as I was to her. So I assumed our newly found friendship was simply platonic. My hope was that I hadn't clumsily damaged our burgeoning closeness.

Habitually, after each ride I anxiously running to the passenger side of the car to do the *gentlemanly* thing for her to exit like I saw on television, I would always walk her to her front door.

After the third time of escorting Lisa to her front door, she surprised me with a quick kiss on the cheek.

Was this her way of showing appreciation or was she beginning to actually like me? Whatever the case, since I had given up making further advances, the kiss immediately resonated a new awareness within me.

I drove home smiling like a fictional Cheshire cat accompanied by a secret erection.

This had to be real!

CHAPTER 3

My parents had never talked to me about dating, sex and other pertinent topics of life. I assumed they figured it was because they felt I was so caught up increasing my educational knowledge that they lacked or just didn't know when or how to discuss the topic with me.

Any and all lessons regarding various obstacles of life were learned from overhearing fellow classmates and watching TV.

Since I lived with mama, who was continually working, I was unaware that she may not have completed or even attended high school.

I knew even less about dad's level of education. I did observe that both were hard workers and constantly strived for the best that life had to offer. Mama was adamant on me going to and completing college.

All I knew was mama, daddy and their families had left the south in order to escape the cruel actions of someone named *Jim Crow*. I often thought whoever he is or was, he must have been a man of great terror and power to have chased them from their homes in Arkansas and Tennessee.

How and when they met, married and later divorced was never explained. I was happy that through it all I maintained a great connection with them both.

As far as Lisa, my first heartthrob, it was always a pleasure seeing her.

One wintery day after class, as I was dropping her off, I got out of the car and opened her door, as I always did. It was then she extended an invitation for me to come in.

Upon entering, she took my coat and hung it in the closet, then proudly gave me a quick tour of the living room that was neatly kept. That was where the tour ended. She said her aunt was in her room and offered me a cup of hot chocolate. Of course, I accepted.

Although it was in my heart I wanted to attempt another kiss, but the thought of being rejected took hold. So, I held back for fear of ruining something with someone I so deeply desired.

Upon leaving, we looked at each other and to my surprise she drew closer and took the lead and thus planted a gentle kiss on my cheek. Then suddenly we were somehow mysteriously drawn to embrace and kiss on the lips. This kiss must have lasted for a good minute or two, which naturally stimulated my *nature* to uncontrollably rise.

This was the beginning of a more intimate relationship with her, which continued for several months.

One day I convinced her to come to where I lived. I wanted her to meet my mother. Mama was very pleased with her and told her to "feel free to visit anytime".

Lisa obviously felt very comfortable in coming over to spend time with mama even when I was not at home. I was strangely ok with that, as I had nothing to hide. Plus, I wanted her in my life more than anyone else. My feeling was that if mama liked her, she must be ok.

I adamantly welcomed unsolicited visits as we became *family*.

One time after getting off my part-time job, as I neared home, I saw a figure of someone waiting out front. The closer I drove I noticed it was Lisa, who had just taken a seat on the door steps. "Wow", what a pleasant surprise. I was just sorry that mama was not home to let her in.

I naturally invited her in and to make herself at home.

After a few moments of kissing, we were passionately driven to uncontrollably go further. Since I was a virgin, I assumed she was too. Sex was awesome!

We had no idea what we were doing, but knew we both enjoyed it. Condoms or birth control was never a topic. We often fulfilled our fantasies by having repeated sex in the hallway, against the bathroom sink and where ever nature took us.

At times, when mama was asleep we would venture to the garage.

Sex became a weekly routine that we both enjoyed.

Finally the inevitable occurred. She told me she had missed her period and was two months past due. She had gone to her doctor who confirmed that she was pregnant.

What would we do? How could I tell mama? How would she tell her mother or aunt with whom she lived?

We agreed that neither of us were ready to bring a child into the world or get married.

We started to grow somewhat apart but still stayed in contact while we tried to figure things out.

Whatever the case, completing school was definitely a priority for us both.

CHAPTER 4

I soon received a partial scholarship to attend a college of my choosing and decided to attend a local university. I chose one close to home so as not to lose connection with family and friends, but also to be close to Lisa and my child to be.

While at the new school I began to get involved in several activities, school and non-school related. One of my non-school activities was taking up various styles of dancing from jazz, modern to African. I became so good in all the styles that I was asked to join a local dance company.

Apparently, I was one of a few artists who could sing and/or dance, depending on the need and was given the opportunity to perform at one of the city's largest public auditoriums.

It was amazing to have opened a show in song before an audience of thousands, I then returned to the stage as a dancer after other artists, and ultimately closed the show with a song.

As a new artist, I was given some billing and advertisement, but not top billing. I was ok with that, as it was not my show. I was grateful for the exposure which feeling as if I had performed at the Apollo or Carnegie Hall.

After my last performance, as I was leaving the dressing room, a guy whom I had seen in school boldly approached me. He was dark complexioned and about my size and height. He then extended his hand.

"Hi, I'm Norman," as he extended his hand for me to shake.

"Hi, I'm Jabarai, nice to meet you," I quickly responded. I was thinking he was probably a talent scout.

As we stood in the rear of the auditorium outside the dressing room, I noticed he continued to smile as he looked me in the eyes as he seemingly gave me the look of inspection from head to toe and repeated the gesture a few times.

As I was beginning to speak, he interrupted and said, "Nice performances, VERY nice."

I graciously continued, "Thank you, do you work here or were you one of the other acts that I may have missed during my wardrobe change?"

"Neither!" he chuckled. "I was in the audience and had to make my way backstage to actually meet you. I've seen you quite often in passing through the school corridors, student lounge and cafeteria."

Although I noticed him in school where there were few blacks, I never gave it a second thought we would end up meeting. Plus, we didn't have any classes in common.

"How did you get pass security, if you don't mind me asking?"

Laughing, he responded "I just acted like I knew where I was going."

Apparently security was preoccupied and simply didn't see him or his ingenious tactics as he probably slithered pass them.

He continued, "I know you're in a hurry to handle some other business and I won't hold you, but do you mind if I have your phone number? I am a musician."

Here, I was a singer and dancer, but not given top billing, why would he want my number?

For obvious reasons of possibly having the opportunity to further my talents, I immediately yielded and gave him my contact information, as requested. As they say, *it's not always what you know, but who you know.*

Also, in passing at school we occasionally felt a connection with the making of the *brother eye contact* between classes.

Having someone to boldly seek me out and approach me was something to which I was completely unaccustomed.

For some reason I continued to question myself about the nature of his introduction.

What did he want with me? Maybe he really was a talent scout who just happened to attend the same university as me.

As we parted and I exited the building, I couldn't help but think *this could be the opportunity I was looking for.* This could be my big break!

Normally, I would be thinking about Lisa or at least stopped by to see her. For some reason all I could think about was the possibility of enhanced opportunities into the entertainment business I loved.

To my surprise Norman called me the next night and soon made his intentions known.

"First let me tell you how impressed I was with your performance. I really liked what I saw."

I quickly responded, "So you are a talent scout?"

He quickly laughed and responded "No" and said that he "had seen me school", but my performance gave him the opportunity to approach and tell me who he was, and how had "always been attracted to me".

Although I was a bit intrigued, I immediately told him I was flattered, but "I'm not gay." I also told him I had a girlfriend.

His response was "that's ok, we can be friends."

Being as that I was not homophobic, I was ok with getting to know him. His being so candid was indeed a plus. Having a close male friend was something I've always wanted.

CHAPTER 5

During one of the many conversations with my new acquaintance, Norman, he discovered that besides dance and gospel music, I also had a passion for other types of music from opera, jazz to R&B.

He often invited me to attend concerts with him which that held at various schools of music throughout the city. Some of the concerts in which he participated he was proud to show his various musical skills, with me as his *special* guest. Others, we attended simply as observers.

I definitely viewed being able to attend these concerts at no cost as a bonus, which most certainly helped to solidify our friendship.

My newly found friendship was blossoming day by day while my relationship with Lisa was gradually diminishing. Good solid male bonding is something most guys desire. I definitely was no exception.

Norman was someone, another male, whose smile lit up like bright Broadway lights every time we were together.

Never once did he reject nor taunt me about my very light complexion, mixed brown and blond curly hair.

In fact, he always complimented me and occasionally stated those were some of my most attractive attributes, as he occasionally spoke of with his intentional hot melting seductive glances from head to toe that I playfully ignored.

I'm not gay, I confirmed to myself. I am a child of God and would never do anything against HIS will. I would have to be steadfast to my understanding of the *word*, as I have been taught.

But somehow Norman's flowery surreptitious advances, especially when he spoke in his sexy baritone voice, was beginning to have an alluring effect on me.

I naturally assumed it was because my voice was a bit high and secretly admired the resonance of each sound he spoke, similarly the way girls and most guys in private always swooned over. I often wondered if it were natural for a guy to admire another guy's voice.

Was this an unexplored part of my psychic or hidden self?

I often wondered how other guys handled these unexplored and unconfessed feelings and admirations, which for reasons unknown to me, guys simply do not openly discuss.

We're typically taught to *suck it in,* be a man and *keep it moving*, as we suppress our deep seated feelings of veneration, or run the risk of being shamefully ridiculed and categorized outside of our manliness.

My church and personal lives were beginning to become more conflicting with each passing day.

Each time Norman and I saw each other, my feelings continued to increase. Surely, this was platonic or was there something more?

At times I wondered was I having a change of sexual preference because of Norman's apparent confession of attraction to me or was this something I needed to experience?

I had to see Lisa in order to secretly and quietly overcome my escalating and possibly erotic feelings toward someone of the same sex.

One call or contact from Norman to meet at a later time or date and I, without hesitation, would immediately cancel any date I may have had with

Lisa, the love of my life and mother of my child to be and undeniable sex partner.

One evening Norman invited me to come over to his house. He wanted me to meet his mother, as well as the rest of his family, if they happened to be home.

Before we got to his home, he asked me to stop the car. He wanted to talk and ask me something, which he said has been on his mind. He didn't want to talk around his family.

He asked me to park about a block from where he lived. I naturally complied.

What was possibly on his mind that he couldn't discuss when we arrived to his home and in front of his mother?

He asked me to look him in the eyes and without any signs of nervousness or hesitation he said very bluntly "We've been hanging out for quite some time and wanted to know if he could date me?"

Needless to say, I was flattered, but somewhat shocked and left speechless. A million thoughts must have crossed my mind which could not have been easily processed at that time.

Before I responded, he continued, "From day one, upon passing you in school and making eye contact, I have been very attracted to you."

Sitting silent for a moment, since he caught me off-guard, I then slowly responded as I searched my thoughts for the best way to nicely answer him without jeopardizing our newly formed camaraderie.

I nervously responded, "I am only interested in friendship. I thought we had that agreement and understanding."

I could sense that he was disappointed at my response, yet tried to appear to be unscathed.

I then told him I had better get home and would meet his mother at a later date.

In spite of my earlier rejection of his bluntness, the next time I saw him in school seemed to have little to no effect on our *bromance*. I assumed he respected my secret yet ambivalent decision.

About a week later he invited me to his home again. This time it was on a Sunday. He was anxious for me to not only meet his mother, but siblings as well whom he knew for sure would be present.

He said his mother was cooking a big meal and wanted to meet me.

For the first time he invited me to the church where he was the Director of Music and organist. He felt this would provide the perfect opportunity to fellowship with his family.

Who was I to refuse a good Sunday home-cooked meal? I graciously accepted the invitation to his church and dinner afterwards at his home with his family. I also accepted his invitation because I knew my mom would be working and most assuredly there would no cooked food at home.

That Sunday morning I arose with eager anticipation of visiting his church and afterwards fellowshipping at his home.

Upon entering the sanctuary, I saw several heads turn in my direction and smile. I assumed everyone knew I was a visitor, as I was obviously a non-member and the only light-complexioned person among the crowd. I momentarily felt as though I was in a foreign land.

I also wondered if I came to the right church or did I inadvertently record the wrong address?

But then I saw Norman as he walked, smoothly from a doorway adjacent to the choir stand and proceeded to the organ. I then knew I was in the right place.

I couldn't help but admire his director's robe that was gathered at each wrist. I assume the gathering was freely permitting him to perform his duties of directing and playing the Hammond organ he had previously told me about, without interfering with the numerous configuration of more than eighty eight keys and knobs.

Church service was awesome. Norman and I sneaked peeks at each other while he was playing the organ and simultaneously directing the choir. He occasionally, winked at me, when able.

At first I was surprised and somewhat embarrassed at the overt flirtation. Then, I thought "Who would know they were aimed at me?" But I accepted them as friendly winks-or did I? A few times I even embarrassingly winked back in acknowledgement.

I was so proud of my new best friend, who just happened to be gay, and demonstration of his musical talents.

At the end of the service everyone held hands and sang an Amen song to confirm its finale.

Norman immediately left his post on the organ and worked his way through the crowd towards me. As he approached, I could see him smiling from east to west, showing all his beautiful white teeth glistening like stars in the night that seemed to become whiter and brighter as he drew closer.

He then introduced me to his sister, who had led the choir in a song--several parishioners and finally the pastor and the first lady. Everyone was exceedingly welcoming beyond expectation.

I immediately told him how I enjoyed the service, which was unlike any other I have ever attended. But then I had to ask myself, was it because of Norman?

I then asked him about his mother, *where was she*? He told me she was at home preparing Sunday dinner and was expecting me.

He then asked, "Are you still coming?"

I quickly responded, "Yes."

We left the church as soon as he received an envelope from a lady whom I didn't meet. I later found out that it was his weekly check for sharing his awesome musical and leadership skills.

Upon exiting the church building, Norman and I walked to my car. He assumed correctly that he could ride with me, as I probably wouldn't know how to easily drive to his home.

After several twists and turns up and down several side streets in unfamiliar territory, we soon arrived to where he lived. Surely, there must have been a shorter route since it was not too far from the church.

I soon discovered through his own admission that he was vying for additional alone time, which seemed to have a positive impression on me.

As we approached his residence, I took notice of the numerous elegant buildings. His building was no exception. It was a big beautiful three story brownstone that looked even more stunning on a Sunday afternoon than before. He led the way toward his second floor apartment.

The closer we got to his apartment, the hungrier I became at the scent of collard greens, cornbread and a mixture of other foods, which was a rarity at my home.

Upon entering his apartment, I was pleasantly overwhelmed by the table setting and the food that his mother had so meticulously prepared and waiting for us to devour. Although, it wasn't Thanksgiving, the amount of food on the table was definitely fit for a king or at least celebration of a special occasion.

He immediately introduced me to the family as his friend from school of whom he had often spoken.

Numerous thoughts began to run through my mind. What had he said about me? What expectations did his family have of me? How was I someone special? Obviously, they had discussed me to some degree or in depth.

Nonetheless, everyone made me feel very much at home and his mother told us to go wash our hands.

I asked him to show me the restroom.

As soon as I commenced to washing my hands and while the water was running, Norman asked me to move over and began to lather his hands with me, as he purposefully touched mine.

I immediately began to inwardly cringe, but didn't resist using the same running water and soap. He then grabbed a towel to dry both of our hands. It was a bit embarrassing, yet exciting.

Noticing my somewhat nervous body reaction he gave me a sly wink and whispered "Shhhhhhh!"

Did he not get the message from his previous attempt or was my passiveness transparent? Plus, what would his family think if they saw him doing this?

I know I may have been a bit naïve, yet again, I was flattered. But since we were at his family's home I didn't want to make a scene. So I let him gently dry my hands along with his. Plus it felt strangely good and as if being catered to by the rich and famous. Something I had only seen done on TV.

It was then confirmed, I was being groomed or *worked*, as the saying goes for something deeper. I've never had such attention from anyone. Not even Lisa.

We proceeded to the dinner table which was awesomely decorated with a fancy table cloth, matching plates and food fit for royalty. Norman's mother was placing the last few cooked items on the table and told me that I could just have a seat while she checked on the homemade dinner rolls.

Norman gently directed me where to sit. Then he quickly sat next to me to keep someone else from taking that space. I assumed it was because I was his *special* guest. By sitting next to me would make the conversation go a lot smoother, particularly knowing I didn't know anyone but him at the table. How thoughtful of him.

When everyone was seated, his older brother by approximately seven years his senior, commenced to blessing the food. Laughter and pleasantries simultaneously filled the air with obviously usual Sunday afternoon dinner discussions about church as various humongous dishes were passed.

His mother sweetly asked, seeing who would answer first. "How was church?"

Norman and his sister simultaneously responded "fantastic". His two brothers had no response to the question, since they were not in service.

I guess in order to engage me in the conversation she decided to ask me my thoughts about the service.

I responded "Service was excellent."

As various dishes were circulating, I noticed each time Norman passed one to me, he made sure he somehow discretely touched my hand or little finger.

Also as we continued to eat, he purposely rubbed his knee on my knee and placed his foot next to mine. Again, here was confirmation that I was being *worked.* He apparently felt somewhat comfortable in doing so with me. He somehow knew I wouldn't *out* him.

He seemed so discreet, yet comfortable with his various *advances* in the rest room and at the dinner table that I began to think maybe this was not his first rodeo. Possibly, his family may have known and accepted his sexual preference for guys, or at least suspected something based on a previous relationship, which we never discussed.

Nonetheless, I enjoyed his company and refused to be intimidated, although I was a bit embarrassed by his numerous concealed gestures.

Besides he knew I wasn't gay nor until recently had the thought ever crossed my mind.

All I knew was that I had not too long ago at the age of about 23 or 24 given up my virginity to Lisa, and was quite satisfied.

Yet, each time Norman and I were together I was beginning to feel a mysterious closeness for another male, particularly him. This was something I had never experienced.

I had to remind myself that this feeling was simply male bonding to the utmost and nothing more.

Anyway, the unsolicited attention I received from Norman was pleasantly stimulating.

After dinner, I thanked Norman's mom for having me over for such a wonderful meal. I then asked him to tell his sisters and brothers, who had departed to other parts of their apartment, that I said goodbye and it was great meeting them.

Norman then agreed to walk me downstairs and to my car. We were just about to exit the building, when Norman gently grabbed my hand and thanked me for coming over.

By the look in his eyes and body language, I think he may have wanted to give me a hug and possibly a kiss but probably felt it was too soon or that he would be rejected. He probably sensed my sudden nervousness. So he gently grabbed my hand for a shake and rubbed my palm with his middle finger.

He walked me to my car and we agreed to see each other the next day in school. He then gave me a goodbye wink and waved as I drove away.

The drive home was filled with numerous mixed emotions and conflicting thoughts. Sensation and contradictory thoughts of the great church service and dinner with his family continued to fill my head.

How I would love to attend each Sunday, but it was a good forty five minute drive from where I lived and not in the best of neighborhoods. If I went there each Sunday, I could spend more quality time with my new best friend. School days simply didn't give us enough time together.

Occasionally, I had to remind him and myself that our relationship could only be platonic.

I assumed his mother cooked a decent meal each Sunday and if I somehow attended church with him I would have a good home-cooked meal after service. But I just didn't want to mislead Norman into thinking this closeness was more than friendship.

As soon as I got home I called Lisa and shared with her the great time I had in church and dinner afterwards.

I started to ask her to attend service with me one Sunday, but decided against it, as I knew she was of another religion that worshipped on Saturday, and Sunday was her day of rest.

CHAPTER 6

The following day I arose and prepared myself for class. For some reason, I was also looking forward to seeing Norman, so I arrived early. The anticipation of running into him that morning was unbelievably high, but the likelihood was low since he attended the music school within the university that was at another location.

Still I arrived early and went to the student lounge where many congregated to chat, study or play cards. I sat in a conspicuous area where I could study and watch for him or be seen by him, if he showed up.

To my disappointment he never appeared during this unscheduled meeting. I proceeded to my first class of the day and was further saddened because I had not seen him, as I had so strangely desired.

Part of me wanted to reiterate to him how I thoroughly enjoyed spending time at his church and dinner with his family. The other part of me wanted to say was that I noticed his subtle advances and remind him that I was straight, but otherwise enjoyed our camaraderie.

Maybe it was fate that I didn't see him, as I didn't want to say anything to jeopardize our rapidly burgeoning bromance. I also wanted to say that he should respect my sexual preference as straight, as I would most certainly respect his.

We didn't see each other that day nor the next, which was probably a good thing. I now had a chance to re-strengthen my relationship with Lisa, which for no fault of hers, seemed to be diminishing.

It was the third day of no contact with Norman before we finally ran into each other at school. Our reunion after a few passing days was so incredibly indescribable, that we instinctively gave each other wide smiles, as the east is from the west, just like the first time I visited his church.

After a few moments of chatting about classes, none of which we had in common, he asked me if I would be able to visit his church again on the upcoming Sunday. I lied and told him I couldn't as I had a date with Lisa.

He then surprisingly told me he too had a girlfriend and that he wanted them to meet. He felt church would be the perfect venue. I agreed, without checking with Lisa, with hope she that would agree. I could now be with my girlfriend and my best buddy.

Since Lisa and I, as of late, had not seen much of each other and were seldom together on Sundays, she promptly agreed to accompany me to Norman's church.

Sunday came and I eagerly picked her up. I was smiling all the way in anticipation of having the best of both worlds. What a pleasant day it would be. The anticipation of spending time with Norman and Lisa at the same time would be amazing. Plus, I looked forward to meeting his girlfriend, whom he had recently mentioned.

Needless to say, church was awesome. I did notice he didn't sneak a wink from the organ, as he did the previous Sunday. I assumed it was because he knew his girlfriend would be watching.

I was occasionally distracted looking around the sanctuary to see if I could determine which one was my best friend's girlfriend.

Suddenly my eyes stopped on someone whom I didn't recognize from the previous Sunday. She was a very attractive young lady about my complexion with freckles. I thought "Could this be her?" Yes, this had to be her?

After service as everyone was hugging, giving greetings and salutations, I watched as

Norman went to the girl I had spotted and brought her to meet me and Lisa.

He said her name was Charlotte. I introduced them to Lisa.

He politely introduced us as he glanced and secretly winked at me when he noticed the girls were exchanging pleasantries. To my surprise and without hesitation, I instinctively returned the gesture.

To my disappointment, he then said they were going to Charlotte's parent's home for dinner and thanked us for attending service.

Although it was not planned, I was hoping that his mother would have prepared dinner and invited us to *break bread* with them. I would have been satisfied to have been invited to accompany them to Charlotte's parent's home.

I was hoping that the four of us could develop a bond and do some double-dating, since Charlotte seemed to be nice, particularly the girls and had similar charm and attractiveness.

As we began to part, Norman softly said to me "we will talk later." Then he gave me his signature *wink*, which I again instinctively returned the signal.

Since Lisa and I had not made dinner plans, she said her mother had cooked and suggested we go there.

CHAPTER 7

The next day as Norman and I saw each other in school, we instinctively and without a care of who may have been observing, came very close to meeting with a unexpected hug and kiss.

Luckily, we quickly composed ourselves and turned the greeting into an acceptable public display of *bromance-level one*, as we hugged with a handshake, then instinctively pulling towards each other with only our forearms separating the bodies.

I told him how nice of a service it was and that it was a pleasure to meet Charlotte.

He then said "Me and Charlotte are dating. Things weren't working out."

"You need to talk to her," I responded.

"She's too clingy," he said, then continued, "I'm not sure if she is who I want."

At that moment, we noticed it was time to head to our separate classes. We both simultaneously said "Let's talk later" as we began to go our separate ways.

But, before we parted company we shook hands, looked each other in the eyes and again instinctively followed up with the *"brotherly"* hug, as he whispered, "Let's meet in the student lounge after our last class, about 3pm." I nervously, but anxiously agreed.

For some reason, my last class was cancelled. I think it was because my instructor may have called in sick and no substitute was available. Therefore I went directly to the student lounge to study as I waited with bated anticipation.

Just after 3pm, someone tapped me on the shoulder. It was Norman, who gently sat next to me as I moved my book bag to the floor. I obviously wanted him and only him to sit next to me.

I thought the conversation would have picked up where it left off. Instead he said, "I need a choir director to help with a choir at church and was wondering if you would be interested?"

I hesitated, "I would be glad to assist, but I've never directed a choir."

"You would be great," he insisted, then continued, "You would have nothing to worry about. I would be working with you and show you what to do. In addition, we could spend more time together as *best* friends."

I thought about it for a quick moment then responded, "I'll give it a try." After all, I did enjoy singing and this would provide the perfect setting to work on my musical skills. I was also honored that he saw something in me that I had never tried.

Somehow, we never talked about his mixed feelings toward Charlotte. All we usually talked about was our mutual admiration for each other, the choir and his appreciation for me and my leadership potential.

At last, I was beginning to have a feeling of belonging to an organization as our *church bond* solidified.

Eventually I was encouraged to lead a song, then another and another. Most time as I led, the congregation would respond with shouts of joy, standing ovations and encores.

I had to remind myself that this gift I was happily sharing wasn't and shouldn't be about me, but the God in me.

Later Norman and I began to sing duets for special services, weddings and other occasions.

We were magically and skillfully being drawn even closer with every song. Occasionally as we were asked to render praises as a duet, we would deliver to the utmost, singing for the Lord while sometime secretly to each other.

It was as if destiny was being fulfilled with each song and glance into each other's eyes for assured support and unrefined confidence.

Unfortunately, the time with Lisa was again beginning to grow more distant as Norman and I spent more time together performing our churchly duties.

Finally one evening after rehearsal, Norman said he wanted to talk.

He started with "We have been spending a quite a bit of time together and I finally know what I most dearly want."

"What"? I responded.

He looked me straight in the eye and said, "YOU."

"Me"?

"Yes, YOU!"

"But Norman, I thought we already talked about this. We've been down this road before. I'm straight and have a girlfriend, whom I'm very happy with. Plus you also have a girlfriend. You just need to work it out."

"I know", he said in his low sexy smooth baritone voice. Then he continued, "You know I have been attracted to you from day one. I've tried to contain myself when around you and even in private, but can't."

I responded, "I must say that I have experienced strange feelings that I find difficult to explain when we are together. I have never dated or even thought about messing around with another guy. *Obviously* you have."

"Yes," he admitted, "but it didn't work out." He continued, "When I saw you on that stage, I knew then that I wanted to get to know you. And if my gut was correct, I felt that you were just the type of person I needed in my life. I knew I had to have you, and for more than a friend."

Being caught off-guard, yet flattered at the same time, I responded "Well, what about your girlfriend, Charlotte?"

"It's not her I want. It's you," He said very adamantly and convincingly. He obviously sensed my ambivalence and was aware of my lack of being homophobic as an opportunity to take our friendship to the next level.

Then he continued, "I will call it quits with her, if you are will to give me a chance."

"Well, I can't do that to Lisa. Plus, as you know she's having my baby."

"If you give me a chance," he begged with total disregard that I was about to be a father. "I promise I will never disappoint you and you can stay with Lisa. But I promise, if you will just give me a chance, you will never be disappointed. Lisa will soon be history, just like Charlotte. Besides, we make music together. We're meant for each other."

"You're absolutely correct in stating we are good friends and make great music together. We are like the Ashford and Simpson of the gospel world."

He then grabbed my hand and leaned toward me, which I did not resist, and gently kissed me on the lips.

He then said, "Was that so bad?"

"No" I responded. But I knew I had just experienced something incredibly unimaginable, yet pleasantly earthshaking. The gentle kiss from another man wasn't as bad as I had imagined. But I also knew I had to take control of myself.

He then went for another. I immediately stopped him.

"What's wrong?" he asked.

"I know what most of you guys do. You go for what you want, a **Mr. Right Now,** then after the newness and excitement wears off, you move on to your next victim." I sternly said, "I will not be anybody's *piece.*"

He gently grabbed my hand, and said "you will never be a *piece.* We have too much vested as best friends."

I thought of the slogan *"Nothing beats a failure but a try,"* so why not! I then responded, "I am willing to give this a try, but let's take this VERY slowly. I really don't know what I'm doing, but what the heck."

I continued "plus, I've always heard that one's lover should be one's best friend. I don't want to lose you as my best friend, all we've accomplished at the church and where our singing could lead."

I've never had anyone to pursue me, so I guess it was the excitement of venturing into something new and hopefully fulfilling.

I began to succumb as he leaned toward me for a second kiss. After the longest and strangest kiss I've ever had which seemingly lasted for a few minutes, he said "I'll be your prince and not a piece, I promise. We will be each other's prince."

During my ride home all I thought about was "What have I done and what about Lisa?" But then I began to smile as I reflected on the long salacious kiss with Norman and our new agreement.

I was always taught that life is about happiness and to be honest, Norman definitely fulfilled that need.

For once I was the pursuee, not the pursuer.

It was a new, yet strange and exhilarating kind of happiness. One of which I was completely unaccustomed.

CHAPTER 8

Finally, after long tedious hours of studying for mid-term exams, our school began the holiday break. I was not in a hurry to go to bed in order to prepare for class.

I made my usual call to Norman to let him know I made it home after spending more quality time with him, my new *bae*, and reflecting on what had occurred.

I could sense the nervousness in his voice as he stated me, "I hope you haven't changed your mind." I assured him that I had not. The conversation started about his attraction toward me and how I overwhelmingly turned him on.

During our numerous conversations, we often transitioned to discussing church and various school activities and how we make a great team.

We found ourselves talking nightly on the phone until sleep overtook us both.

Since school was closed, we knew we probably wouldn't see each other until Thursday night's choir rehearsal. We made our usual plans to meet at church early to go over songs that we would teach. Thursday seemed so far in the distant.

As each conversation became more erotically heated, I found myself having thoughts about him. I never imagined awakening in the middle of the night having to change my underwear and/or sheets due to a *wet dream* or two.

After the second night of wet dreams and having to change sheets, I finally decided to place a towel between me and the bottom sheet for obvious reasons. It worked!

When Thursday finally came around I rushed to the church, and arrived early with bated anticipation of seeing Norman. Yes, I wanted to see the choir members, but to see Norman would be the highlight. Because I arrived earlier than scheduled, I had to wait until he came to open the door.

As soon as he unlocked the church door, he immediately locked it behind us to prevent anyone from witnessing the long salacious kisses.

We immediately began to hug and kiss so hard as if squeezing the juice from an orange.

The anticipation of seeing him again, coupled with the nervous nightly romantic discussions seemingly had strong erotic affects, which led me to unstoppable wet dreams.

I often thought was this love or sex? Or was it simply something new for me that I had heard other guys had tried but rarely discussed?

Due to surprise inclement weather and fewer choir members showing up, rehearsal was short.

It had begun to snow heavily so he asked me if I wanted to spend the night. I told him yes, but I would have to call mama to let her know. She agreed, as she didn't want me driving in the storm.

She then asked to talk to Norman's mother to assure they were in mutual agreement. For my safety, I was nervously happy that our mothers agreed, although they had never met or even had a phone conversation.

Norman's mother made sure I felt comfortable and stressed that I could address her as mom and she would officially be my *other* mother. Needless to say, this most definitely made me feel at home.

Norman led me to the room where he slept which had two twin beds with mix matched spreads and somewhat flattened pillows, as if they were years old and had never been discarded for newer ones.

Nonetheless, everything seemed very clean. The room had no door, but only a curtain of seemingly old material which parted in the middle to yield reasonable privacy.

My *other mother* approached us saying "Be sure to wash up before going to bed."

She continued, "Jabarai, I promised your mother I would look out for you as if you are my own, and I will."

After washing up and preparing myself for the night, numerous thoughts and visions began to fill my head. Thoughts such as, was his family as nice as they appeared? Would he attempt to touch me during the night? And if he did, since I had never been sexual with another male, how would I respond?

This was the first time spending the night away from home, except as a child or visiting a relative, so the feeling was a bit disconcerting.

Before taking my assigned bed, Norman and I sat up and talked a long time, as if we hadn't talked in months.

Prior to retiring for the night, he first checked on his mother and the rest of the family to make sure they were in bed or at least settled in their own rooms. He was obviously checking to see if the coast was clear prior to attempting his next move.

He then returned to the room, grabbed my hands and quickly but gently pulled me to him and gave me a kiss with equal or more passion than he did the previous time.

As we continued to kiss and embrace, I could feel his erected lump of a *manhood* through my underwear.

Being as that we were both well-endowed, we wore jockey underwear or jockstrap to help prevent others from knowing what was secretly underneath.

It could be quite embarrassing for others to become fixated on what's below the waist, particularly church folk of both sexes.

We of course had to remove our *daily restraints* prior to going to bed.

I must admit, I was a bit ashamedly curious as to what he was hiding, but I didn't want it known.

This was definitely a feeling that was new to me, which felt extremely strange, yet mysteriously good. As I reflected, I'm sure he was likewise curious.

After the removal of our under restraints and put on the pajamas that his mother had provided, we instinctively resumed our positions of hugging and kissing.

Suddenly we heard a loud popping sound, which caused me to push away from him.

The only thing I could think was either we had been caught or it was the sound of someone approaching.

He obviously saw the look of terror on my face. He said, "That's nothing to worry about. It was only the sound of a mousetrap being triggered."

It was then that others in the family arose looking around and asking each other, "Where is it?" As if they had struck gold.

Then they headed pass his bedroom in search of the sprung trap that so rudely interrupted our embrace.

He grabbed his robe and handed me his spare so as to hide our obvious erections wouldn't be visible to the family.

We joined the family in search of the sprung mousetrap. I heard his little sister yell that she found it.

He then fearlessly grabbed it, showed it to everyone and proudly tossed the dead mouse out the back door and over the fence. He then rebaited, reset the trap and washed his hands.

Everyone reconvened to their separate sleeping quarters.

As he and I returned, I told him that this mouse thing was something new to me. Just the thought of rodents in the apartment was a definite mood breaker. By then our erected penises had receded, which was probably a good thing.

Had it not been for the mouse, who knows how far we would have ventured with the risk of being caught by his mother or another family member in an embarrassing or uncompromising position.

We gave each other a quick kiss as we retreated to our separate twin beds. He then assured me that everything was ok. He did mention that he was embarrassed that they had occasional rodents, but they have never entered the bedroom and to sleep well.

Throughout the night I could seemingly hear strange sounds of mice running between the walls.

How I wanted either to sleep in the same bed with him, out of fear of being bitten, as if the mice wouldn't attack him or go home to my safer haven.

When I finally fell asleep, I was awakened sometime that morning with Norman looming over me. He then gently kissed my lips.

"Time to get up" he said, "Mother is preparing breakfast."

I said "What time is it?"

He responded "It's 8am and don't think you're going anywhere. Take a look outside."

"Oh my God, look at all the snow," I replied. "I need to call home."

He led me to the phone where I immediately called and reluctantly reported in. Mama understood and told me to be safe. I assured her I would check in later.

Luckily, it turned warmer thus melting the snow to the point where the streets seemed safe enough to journey home.

I then prepared to return home about 3 pm. Norman told me I didn't have to leave, but I left anyway. I then said my goodbyes to the family as he walked me down the stairs while gently kissing me at the bottom landing prior to exiting the building.

During my drive home, I reflected on the events of the previous night. The embrace and passionate kiss and feel of the touching and hardness of our *manhood* through our underwear and how I had succumbed, made me secretly smile.

I also began to think since he felt so comfortable and was brazen enough to kiss in his mother's home that he must have done it before.

I again wondered if his family, particularly his mother, was aware of his sexual preference. What would she have done if she caught us kissing?

One thing I knew for sure was that my mother would never tolerate any type of same-sex affection, particularly in her home. Thus, I never shared with her the unsolicited, yet developing forbidden closeness that I was becoming comfortable with.

CHAPTER 9

The more Norman and I were together either in school or at church, the more natural our relationship felt.

I often wondered if anyone could sense our heightened level of affection towards each other.

Did they think it was simply the closeness of best friends or were we more transparent than I imagined? Would it make a difference? I'm sure everyone has a story to tell or hidden skeleton in their closet, even church folk.

We often visited various church members after service and visibly became known as an *item*. Whenever someone invited one of us over or to a party or impromptu social gathering, an invitation was automatically extended to the other.

At this point Norman and I still had not engaged sex, we often managed to sneak a hot kiss or affectionate touch behind closed doors, or under a table while playing cards, during dinner or simply in passing.

We often acted as if we were two kids playfully and joyfully enjoying sneaking to do the forbidden, as children often do.

Finally, one evening when leaving someone's home, he asked me to pull over to a secluded side street which was adjacent to several empty lots and partially torn down buildings to park to talk.

He discussed how he wanted to become more intimate. I momentarily hesitated, but then I agreed that I too was feeling the urge. Then I said "I have no idea where to go to consummate our intimate relationship."

We knew that either of our places was out of the question, particularly at mama's home. He admitted we had a better chance at his place, but we wanted total privacy without fear of being caught.

The only thing that ran through my mind was, if either of us were of the opposite sex, being caught wouldn't be much of a problem, as that would typically be accepted or tolerated.

I knew that running the risk of being ostracized by family and or friends would be totally incomprehensible.

While parked, I turned the engine off in order to save gas while we commenced to talking as we held hands, which lasted for about a minute.

Suddenly, as we began to stare each other in the eyes we began to kiss lightly with each kiss becoming more intense.

Then before we knew it, like wild animals in a heat of passion, we instinctively continued kissing, rubbing, touching and instinctively began to undress each other to the point of semi-nudity.

This must have continued for several minutes, possibly longer, as we lost track of time and place. I noticed the windows became fogged to the point of semi-complete darkness, with the exception of the light illuminating from the full moon.

With our pants and underwear down to our knees, we continued our moment of passion. This was the first time we saw and touched each other's manhood. The more we touched and kissed, the more *heated* we became. There was no stopping. For some reason, we felt safe in this virtually desolate area.

Suddenly the light became rather bright on the driver's side. It was a flashlight shining through the completely window followed by several taps.

It was a lone policeman who told us to "open the door and get out."

We scurried as much as we could to pull up our pants and button our shirts. We knew for sure we would be handcuffed, arrested, taken to jail and our parents notified.

The officer asked us for identification; then, told us to get back in the car. We of course followed his orders.

To our surprise the cop said "You guys need to be more careful."

We knew for sure he was going to call for backup or handcuff us and haul us off to jail.

How would we explain this to our parents?

Then surprisingly, we noticed he started groping and rubbing himself. He ordered us to pull our pants down and kiss.

We nervously complied as he pulled out his manhood and began to masturbate while watching us.

After a few long minutes we noticed he began to breathe hard, then subsequently climaxed on the ground next to the car.

After reinserting himself back into his pants, he said "I'm going give you guys some good advice. The next time you feel horny, don't park on the street. Get a room. Now go, and don't let me see you guys again like this."

We nervously drove away saying how lucky we were as we vowed there would never be a repeat of a situation like that.

As the saying goes, we definitely *dodged a bullet*. We might not be so lucky as to find a gay cop or one that was a bit freaky or sympathetic enough to release us.

We also discussed that what had just happened could only have happened in the movies and not have been real. Yet it was! Scary and kinky, but very real!

CHAPTER 10

Upon arriving home I nervously called Lisa, as it had been more than a week since we had spoken. I knew her voice would be soothing and possibly put me back on track.

How I wanted to confess to her my unnatural closeness to Norman, but then I was afraid of losing her for good. Leading a double life was definitely new, challenging and a bit frightening.

I ultimately decided I had to come clean with myself and handle this on my own while still associating myself with Norman, but only at church.

I purposely did everything I could do to avoid Norman when classes resumed the following week. I knew his route and intentionally took different paths to various classes.

I also avoided our usual meeting spot, the student lounge. I accepted no calls from him at home. But then there was no avoiding him while at church. I was now the main choir director and felt compelled to attend Thursday night's choir rehearsal.

Rehearsal was a bit tense. Since Norman and I had not met to discuss new music, I decided we should review songs from the past and I would quickly make my exit.

After rehearsal, as I was trying to leave I tried to not look him in the eye. To my dismay, he caught up with me.

"What's wrong?" He asked with the look of hurt.

"Nothing!"

"We need to talk." He further insisted.

I reluctantly said "ok."

He asked me to wait for him.

For inexplicable reasons, I simply couldn't turn him down.

I agreed to take him home as his sister took the family car. We talked about my obvious distance from him and not answering his calls.

While enroute to his home, I told him "I was deeply afraid at what had happened with the police the other night."

He expressed that he felt the same, grabbed my hand, kissed it and told me that he loved me and reassured me it would never happen again. He thought the area was safe.

I said "You got that right. Do you know what could have happened if that cop was on the *straight and narrow*? That was the worse situation I have ever encountered. "

He agreed and repeated as he did before, "That definitely will not happen again."

He said he wanted to see me again, but this time we would get a room, like the officer had advised.

As I pulled up in front of his house, he leaned toward me puckering his thick luscious lips as he went for a kiss.

"NO," I reluctantly, but adamantly responded as I pushed him away.

"Please come in," he begged. "My mother has been asking about you."

I momentarily hesitated, then agreed, as she was my self-proclaimed *other mother*.

As we entered the downstairs front door, he surprisingly grabbed me and gave me a kiss passionate enough to recharge a dead battery. We both then knew I could no longer resist him.

While still on the lower landing, I asked "What do you want with me? Besides, maybe the incident with the cop was a sign from God that this lifestyle is not for us." I continued.

"Do you know if he could have unlawfully enforced his authority and made us perform sexual acts with him rather than with each other?"

Yes, we could have reported him had he made us have sex with him, but that would have opened another can of worms.

He could have easily flipped the script by taking us into jail anyway, denying his freaky acts. Who would the judge believe?"

"You're right. But that didn't happen."

He continued, "Although this was not my first involvement with another man, I somehow feel you are meant to be my soulmate. I simply cannot let you get away.

I know who I want and what love is. I love you."

CHAPTER 11

It was obvious I could no longer resist his persistent advances. I continually unsuccessfully searched myself for the appropriate expression or words to define this overwhelming fondness for Norman.

I often asked myself "What was this uncanny feeling I had deep within that was so irresistible about Norman?" Or "why did I allow him to kiss, hold and touch me?" "I was quite satisfied with Lisa, or was I?"

I've always heard that if you ever let someone of the same sex touch you, you would know immediately if *same sex love* was innate or not.

I've also heard that no one can satisfy another like someone of the same gender. Once tried, it would be difficult to go back.

I can honestly say the feeling I had developed for him was completely unsolicited and unexpected. Definitely like no other. It took me to the mountain top and there I wanted to stay.

What an awesome feeling! The same rush I would imagine one receives when being urged to go zip lining, bungee jumping or for an amazing breathtaking ride at an amusement park.

I had to give it a try.

CHAPTER 12

Norman and I decided to follow the officer's advice and take the next step of finally getting a hotel room.

It was a fleabag of a hotel that was near his home that charged by the hour.

I asked, "How do you know of this place?"

"I've heard about it." He smoothly responded.

I didn't ask further questions, thus assuming he had used the hotel in the past or had heard about it from the streets.

We decided to split the cost and rent four hours of usage.

Being still on the *down low* and renting a hotel room with a guy was rather embarrassing. I tried as best I could to avoid eye contact with the desk clerk.

As we entered the room, I immediately noticed an old lamp which sat on top of a scratched up night stand.

As I looked further, there was an obviously *well-used* mattress that laid on top of some coils for a box spring that seemed to be attached somehow to the legs of the bed. The semblance of a headboard was rusted old iron and not well connected to the bed. Nevertheless, we finally had privacy to *explore.*

Upon closing the door and making sure it was locked, we began to kiss and gradually undress each other in our *safe sanctuary* to the point of complete nudity.

For the first time we saw each other from head to toe without a stitch of clothes on as we momentarily backed away a few inches, then about two feet to admire each other's physique.

We instinctively then began to mechanically, yet romantically touch and massage each other's hands, arms, shoulders and chest. We wanted to take our time to admire and gently explore. Plus we had four hours for rented bliss to comfortably review without fear of being caught.

After a few tender moments we began to embrace without handling each other's penises, which seemed to clumsily stab each other below the stomach with rock hard unyielding.

Still being vertical, we instinctively returned to kissing and subsequently falling back on the bed, which unexpectedly sank in the middle.

We chuckled a bit succumbing to the sunken bed, which momentarily suspended the intensity. We then immediately resumed our time of uninterrupted rented hours of passion.

After a seemingly short time period which could have lasted to dawn, we heard a knock at the door.

"Who is it?" Norman asked.

"Your time is up in fifteen minutes." the voice responded, then continued, "If you want more time, please see the desk clerk."

"Ok, thank you." Norman responded.

We simultaneously responded, "That was quick." As we chuckled!

We looked at each other as we heard footsteps fading to notify other patrons.

Then I told him "As much as I'd like for us to pay for more time, I'd better be going." As I definitely didn't tell mama I would probably be home late or who I was with. I didn't want her to worry.

We quickly got dressed giving each other a final kiss and nightly embrace prior to exiting the room for four hours of bliss well-spent.

As we left the hotel lobby and again feeling rather embarrassed, I purposely tried not to make eye contact with the front desk clerk. Giving away our secret and what had occurred was something I wanted to avoid.

The ride to Norman's home was filled with joy, laughter, holding hands and further confession of our love for each other.

We then agreed to give up having girlfriends and concentrate on each other.

I had finally found love. One that I didn't have to chase, but one that was definitely chasing me. The chase was over.

CHAPTER 13

Although we still were not *out of the closet* with the nature of our newly committed relationship, everyone knew we were quite close.

My guess is many may have secretly suspected something lascivious was occurring.

Respecting the church and its fire and brimstone teachings were constantly on my mind. I had to justify what I was now doing. After all as it is stated in the bible, "He who is without *sin*, let him cast the first stone. Or were we really sinning?

Love is love and we were both consenting adults.

One Sunday upon leaving church, a nice elderly lady from the Mother's Board, by the name of Mother Williams, invited us to her home for dinner.

This likewise gave us the opportunity to continue the fellowship and camaraderie development with the Williams family, which included her sixteen year old son, Ricky, Mrs. Williams' mother and other church members who were a part of a small clique. We of course accepted.

Soon after our first D.L. date at Mother Williams' home, which became the after church gathering spot for a great meal followed by hours of playing various board and card games. We drew even closer.

Not only was Mother Williams a great cook, but loved to talk and no room was off limit. She always made sure everyone was comfortable.

My guess is not only was she very giving, but also very lonely being as that she had no husband. She seemingly enjoyed the company of other men around the house. Norman and I helped to fulfill that need.

Mother Williams' son, Ricky, was quite cute and somewhat effeminate, which Norman and I discussed that he would probably be gay one day. He became more like a little brother to us, but we made sure our personal lives were never discussed with him. We did not want to be an influence, but let him develop naturally whichever way he would go.

One day after church, we went over to Mrs. Williams' home as we customarily did. Ricky, who was quite astute and friendly, particularly to me, pulled me aside and showed me a note that he found under his pillow from Norman.

The note said:

"You're very cute and I find myself attracted to you. Call me later but don't tell anyone."

Norman

He said he didn't know what to do and for unknown reasons, he felt he could trust me and had to share. He then let me know how uncomfortable the note made him feel.

Since I was the newest member to the church as well as to the Williams' family, I quickly thought, "Why did he choose to confide in me?"

The only reasons I could think of why he confided in me was that he liked how I directed the choir and we had similar openly receptive and happy personalities. We were very much like brothers.

I told him to ignore the note. Rip it up and tell no one, which he said he would comply. I didn't want to get Norman in trouble, as we were becoming like family to the Williams.

God knows what would have happened if his mother had seen and interpreted the note way me and little Ricky did.

But that may have been a sign that Norman was *possibly* up to something lewd and lecherous with young Ricky in mind.

I began to think to myself, "Now that Norman had managed to convince and convert me, was he now planning his next victim or was this all a thoughtless mistake?"

Jealousy was never my nature, nor had he ever given me a reason to be.

If his intentions were guiltless in leaving Ricky the note, why would he leave such a message? Why had he not discussed it with me, if he was jokingly innocent?

Nonetheless, I never mentioned the note to Norman. I wanted to see what, if anything would unfold and was I *really* his prince or piece. Was I his *Mr. Right* or *Mr. Right Now*? Only time would tell if he were seeking to convert Ricky for his secret *side piece*.

As Ricky and I became closer with each encounter, he occasionally secretly mentioned in private that no more notes were left.

Possibly Norman was up to something of an immoral nature with Ricky in mind. If so, he may not have thought about the consequence of losing me, but also the word getting out to Mrs. Williams and subsequently to the church.

CHAPTER 14

One Sunday afternoon after leaving church, Mrs. Williams invited me and Norman to her home for holiday festivities. The following day was the Columbus Holiday and she wanted to make sure we all got together again to celebrate, as we did for any occasion.

Norman and I were about to leave when Ricky pulled me aside and said that since he didn't have school the next day if he could spend the night with me. Yes, it caught me off guard, but I told him if his mother was ok with it, I would be too. I also informed him that I would have to check with my mother for permission.

Both our moms agreed, but Ricky would have to sleep in the spare bedroom since my older brother had married and moved out.

Ricky quickly gathered a few items and we took Norman home. It was a bit strange that Norman and I couldn't hold hands while taking him home, particularly with Ricky in the back seat.

A goodbye kiss was definitely out of the question as we wanted our private lives to remain that way.

Upon arriving to my home, I of course introduced mom to my new little *play brother*.

Although the next day was a holiday, she was preparing herself for bed and work the following morning. She could have taken off, but was being paid double time for having agreed to go in.

Mom asked us to not make too much noise, as she had to get up by 4am.

I showed Ricky where he would be sleeping and helped him get settled in. We then went downstairs to watch television, but keeping the volume low.

We finally went to bed about 3am. I'm sure mom left the house as scheduled about 4:45am.

About 5am I felt my bed move. Surely it was the result of me going into R.E.M. of sleeping or dreaming and going into a deep sleep after a full day. Ricky obviously had not fallen asleep and heard momma leave and crawled into my bed.

"What are you doing here?" I asked.

"I'm scared and can't fall asleep. Can I sleep with you?" He responded.

"Sure, just stay on your side." I playfully, yet seriously answered.

Shortly afterwards as I was almost back asleep, I noticed as he turned over he moved a little closer toward the center.

Suddenly I was slightly awakened by the touch of fingers softly and carefully moving on my side heading toward my early morning erect penis. Surely, this had to be a dream. But it wasn't.

I decided to try and ignore the subtle movements with sleepy grunts of being disturbed which momentarily stopped the crawling fingers.

Soon the crafty fingers inched their way and boldly began rubbing my fully erected penis which had begun to throb for attention.

"Ricky, what are you doing?" I angrily yelled. "Now roll back over to your side of the bed or go back to your own bed and get some sleep."

"I'm sorry." He said in an extremely pitiful tone as he quickly turned over with his back facing my back.

I'm sure he felt embarrassed at the fact that I did not respond as he wished to his young tender advances.

Although the touch of someone rubbing my manhood felt good, I was determined to keep our brotherhood and friendship platonic. Besides, he was only sixteen and I was committed to Norman.

After finally getting up, he again apologized for what he had attempted and with his big beautiful light brown eyes pleaded for me to not tell his mother. I agreed! That would be our secret.

He then further confided in me that he felt he was attracted to guys and thought he would try to explore his feelings with me, which was the basic reason he wanted to spend the night. He also sincerely confessed that he thought I was attractive and was hoping I felt the same.

I told him I appreciate the compliment, but I looked at him like a little brother and if I were to join him in his *experiment*, it would ruin our friendship. Plus, he was too young.

He agreed and asked me again to not tell his mother or anyone else. I confirmed our earlier agreement.

The following Sunday it was a bit unsettling to see him in church or at his home, but being a young man of my word, my promise was kept.

Being that no feathers appeared to be ruffled between me and his family, I likewise assumed he never told his mother or anyone else what he attempted.

He could have easily *turned the table* by lying, saying I tried to touch him, which would have opened up a can of worms. He apparently didn't. Thank God.

That was the last time I let him spend the night with me and the last time it was discussed.

CHAPTER 15

As a result of my new unrefined weakness, Lisa and I were continuing to grow more distant. Norman had obviously been successful in taking my whole heart from her although I still treasured the friendship.

The thought of her having my baby seldom crossed my mind. Most of the time, my thought about her was if and when she would have an abortion, since neither of us was ready for parenthood. I promised I would pay to have the fetus aborted and thus have total freedom to explore my new lifestyle.

During one of our infrequent conversations, Lisa told me she had gone to the doctor and was told the time for an abortion had passed, so she had attempted to self-abort.

"How did you attempt it?" I asked.

"I tried drinking some bathroom cleaner, then punching myself in the stomach."

I then began to feel guilty, yet sorry and concerned. I didn't want her to do any harm to herself or cause an abnormality to the fetus. It was then that I realized that I somehow still cared for her. She said she had to try something.

I asked her "if I needed to come over?" She emphatically said "**NO!**"

"I'm coming anyway and will see you in a few minutes." I immediately hung up. My caring for her was confirmed.

I couldn't get dressed fast enough. Seemingly a million thoughts crossed my mind.

I wanted to hug her and tell her that although I still cared, I simply wasn't ready to be a father, least of all to get married."

How would I tell mama who had no idea of Lisa's pregnancy?

How would she explain it to her mother or aunt with whom she lived?

I wanted to tell Lisa of my involvement with Norman, but somehow couldn't find the words or the nerves.

The closer I got to her place the more nervous I became. I was praying that she didn't do anything to harm herself or the fetus, particularly to the point of being deformed.

I was hoping she would let me in.

After several minutes of ringing her doorbell and frantically knocking on her door, she finally let me in.

"So how are you?" I asked.

"I'm ok." She reluctantly continued, "After drinking the bathroom cleanser and punching myself in the stomach, my abdomen began to swell, but it went down."

"Thank God you're ok, but maybe you need to see the doctor to check on the fetus."

"I said I'm ok and so is the fetus. Now will you please leave?"

As I approached her for a hug, she backed away and told me "Now will you please leave, I can handle this on my own."

I told her that we did this together and if the fetus did not somehow abort after all she had insanely attempted, she would not have to go through the pregnancy nor the parenthood alone.

I then pleaded with her to please see another doctor and I would pay.

That suggestion was quickly rejected. We even discussed her seeing a *street doctor* from the *hood* to help her abort.

We quickly came to the conclusion that an illegal removal of the fetus would be too dangerous and could possibly kill her. She knew then that she was not totally abandoned. We hugged and cried.

Finally, I left when she assured me she would not try to self-abort again or attempt any harm to herself.

How would I work things out in choosing between Lisa and Norman? I knew somehow there had to be resolution.

As Norman and I continued our romantic relationship, my focus toward Lisa lessened. I started to slowly re-implement the *out of sight, out of mind* phrase as the situation would somehow slowly take care of itself.

CHAPTER 16

Norman and I continued to solidify our relationship by us spending weekends together at his mother's home.

Unbeknownst to his mother, or maybe not, and the rest of his family, we attempted quick interludes of touching and kissing. When he thought it was safe, he would often crawl into the bed assigned to me.

If I felt like cuddling for a few minutes, I would do likewise with him. Either way we always found ourselves proceeding to kiss.

Kissing often led to quite a bit of muffled frotting and keeping a towel handy for an easy clean up. We kept our pajamas or underwear nearby, in case we had to make a quick separation.

Our ears were constantly on guard for someone who would awaken to use the restroom or go for a nightly drink of water.

On a few occasions following some intense lovemaking we mistakenly fell asleep in each other's arms.

Holding each other after each nervously muffled climax was extremely relaxing and reassuring.

Whatever the case, we made sure not to become too complacent and made sure we retreated back to our individual twin beds before morning.

One morning after a few hours of passion, we heard someone walking down the narrow hallway towards our room. Norman quickly, but quietly moved to his side of the room, just in case someone wanted to separate the *privacy curtains* in place of a door to check on us.

I often wondered if someone quietly separated the curtain to check on us while we were embraced. To our knowledge, thankfully no one did!

After a few close moments and fear of being caught, we decided we would get an apartment together. We were both in our early twenties and we needed full privacy and security of being alone.

In addition to the work-study program at school, I decided to take on an additional job in order to responsibly handle my end of the bargain.

Since Norman already received a good salary as a church musician, we knew that his financial end of our agreement would be sufficient.

Because of something negative on his credit report, as I was told, I had to get the apartment solely in my name.

The first few months together were awesome, but then I noticed how lazy he was around the house and living together began to get rather tense. He seemingly never wanted to help clean or cook. But the sex was so good that our house sharing differences seemed to be unimportant.

Soon he started to delay paying his portion of the rent. He continually managed to come up with excuse like, personal bills or lending money to a family member.

When confronted about our *joint obligation and agreement,* he suddenly snapped in a way I've never seen him.

"What I do with my money is my business," he angrily hollered.

"Yes, it is. But we have an agreement, and you're not keeping your end of it." I quickly responded.

The argument suddenly became physical when he took a swing at me with something he was holding. I quickly ducked.

The item he attempted to hit me with left a dent in the closet door. We continued to fight until he stormed out of the apartment. He probably realized then that although I was easygoing, I was not going to be an easy *pushover* nor would I stand for any type of abuse.

All I could think about was the phrase, *you never know a person until you live with them.*

He returned within the hour and apologized. He knew how much I loved him. After all, I had left my girlfriend for him. He skillfully converted and stole me from my first love, Lisa.

He also knew I couldn't resist his charm and warm embrace. So we made up with hours of more passionate uninhibited love. Whatever we imagined, we tried, often leaving us pleasantly laughing, smiling and going for another round of hot togetherness.

A few months later, I happen to arrive home a bit early and noticed him whispering on the phone. He obviously heard me enter, and was trying to end the conversation by taking the call to the restroom.

As I listened closely, I could tell he was planning a date with someone. I continued to eavesdrop. I could easily tell that the *someone* he was whispering to happen to be Charlotte, his ex-girlfriend.

When confronted about the conversation, he said it was all my imagination and that he was talking with his mother, who was having problems.

Although I didn't refute his statement, I knew it was an obvious lie, but would wait to see the outcome on the night of the planned date.

The next night, he told me he had to go to his mother's house to help her with something. I offered to go with him.

"No, that's alright," He responded.

I felt he was probably up to something with his ex-girlfriend. When he left our apartment, I waited about an hour and called his mother.

"Are you ok?" I asked.

"Yes. Why do you ask?" She responded.

"Well Norman said that you had a situation you needed help with, so I was just checking."

By then I was becoming upset at Norman's intentional deception.

"Have you seen Norman?" I asked.

She told me Norman and Charlotte had been there.

"Where did they go?" I continued to probe.

"He told me they were going to Zion Baptist Church on Madison Ave." She responded.

"Thank you."

By then I was furious, at the fact that he had lied and was out with his ex, even if it was at church.

Although, I really didn't mind him being friends with her or anyone else, I was angry at the deception. Plus further breaking of the trust and agreement we had to leave our girlfriends alone. It wasn't fair to us or them.

As I continued to *fume* over his double dealing, I couldn't resist the urge to get in my car and catch him in the act, but my keys were mysteriously missing.

I looked all over our apartment, then realizing Norman probably took my keys so I couldn't look for him. What he hadn't anticipated was that I had a spare set.

The closer I got to the church, the more I fumed over his obvious deception. He intentionally broke the trust which I had developed for him. He had violated what I had considered true friendship, male bonding and the love I had developed for him.

All I could think of was how he had relentlessly stormed into my life, slowly convinced me to leave Lisa and introduced me to a lifestyle I would find difficulty giving up. I simply couldn't release-HIM! I was hopelessly in love with him and there was no turning back.

As I entered the church, I noticed him sitting about four rows from the rear with his right arm around Charlotte's back as he gently caressed and rubbed her shoulder.

I beckoned an usher to get his attention. When he saw it was me, I could see the fear and nervousness in his eyes. He had been caught red-handed.

As he exited the sanctuary entering into the dimly lit narthex, he immediately started giving excuses and begging for forgiveness. The more he pleaded the angrier I became.

"Where are my keys?" I asked.

"Oh, I mistakenly took them when I grabbed mine."

This obvious lie made me more intensely heated with anger. He was obviously attempting to cover up his act of deceit. I could feel a frustration and jealousy like never before.

Suddenly, without respect for the church, I inexplicably without restraint slapped him so hard, that he fell against the wall.

I had begun to lose it and didn't care who heard the commotion. I continued to slap and hit him in a way that surprised us both. An uncontrollable rage had overcome my typical gentle nature.

The usher who got his attention for me in the sanctuary, followed by his ex-girlfriend immediately rushed out to see what was going on.

As he was a guest artist for the evening he had to protect his image.

I had occasionally heard about similar incidences occurring in the house of God, but never thought I would be a contributant.

"Nothing, I'm ok." He quickly stated. "I just tripped over the rip in the tile and fell against the wall."

The usher returned to the sanctuary to resume his duties.

I told Norman to step outside. We needed to talk. As we exited the narthex, his ex-girlfriend followed.

"What's going on?" She innocently asked.

"What going on is me and Norman are in a relationship and have been for some time."

Still startled, she asked Norman, "WHAT? Is that true?"

He was completely speechless, as he never expected me to *out* him, which was likewise a surprise to me.

As we continued to stand outside the church, I angrily confessed all of our business to her and that we were more than good friends.

I continued, "We were very sexual in a way that you couldn't imagine."

She seemingly didn't believe me.

"Tell her," I demanded. "Tell her--Tell her or you haven't felt half of my anger!"

I wanted her to know how he persistently and relentlessly courted me until I converted. He had never seen me lose my temper, which he knew was quite uncharacteristic.

We must have been outside for quite some time, when we noticed church was dismissing.

He said "Let's get in the car."

The two of them got in front seat of his car, while I got in the back.

"You're going to take her home NOW." I demanded.

Without provocation from her, but still filled with anger and seemingly temporary insanity, I vindictively snatched off her hairpiece as if she were my nemesis, jumped out of the backseat and said to Norman "I had better see you at **OUR** apartment in one-half hour."

Then I continued," Better yet, I am going to follow you to make sure you take her straight home."

Whatever they talked about while I wasn't in the car, I really didn't care. All I knew was I came to get my man and there would be no *if's and's or but's*.

Upon returning home I thought of how I had literally lost my mind, but how Norman had driven me to it. I said it would never happen again and was thoroughly determined that it was over between us.

I told myself, "How I wish I had not taken my anger out on Charlotte. She was completely innocent." But the damage was done. Nonetheless, I was determined to get my man back.

As we entered the apartment there was a stillness that filled the air. We looked at each other for a few tense minutes without uttering a word.

He broke the silence by apologizing for misleading me. I followed up by apologizing for my outburst at church and for **outing** him.

"If you want us to date girls, it would have been ok, but we have to be open and honest with each other." I continued. "You coerced me to give up Lisa and here you are spending time with Charlotte."

"No, I'm done with girls. I made a mistake. All I want is you. I love you and only want to be with YOU." He emphasized.

Without hesitation, "I love you too." We then hugged, kissed and resumed to our usual night of uninterrupted passion. But this time it seemed to be better than ever as we explored each other's bodies seemingly as never before.

We began to laugh at my outburst at church and the incident with Charlotte. We cried and apologized to each other until falling asleep.

CHAPTER 17

Weeks passed as we continued our happy home/school/church relationship. He even began to responsibly handle his share of the bills, which made life a lot easier.

I hadn't heard a peep from Lisa and I assumed Norman had likewise severed his contact with Charlotte.

Then one afternoon I again came home early from work. He obviously didn't hear me enter. Suddenly he started whispering. His whispering of course encouraged my interest and inquisition.

"So who are you suddenly whispering to?"

"My mother" He replied.

I playfully grabbed the phone and said "Hello mom."

"No, this is not his mother." The voice on the other end responded.

I could tell it was his ex and handed him the phone back and said "When you're done with that bitch, we need to talk." I wanted her to hear every word.

Even though I knew it took two to tango, he had to have been secretly courting her without my knowledge and against our reconfirmed agreement.

When he got off the phone, he told me he was moving back home with his mother and that he and Charlotte had decided to get married. He had proposed to her a few weeks ago.

"You can leave now. I knew it was too good to be true and that you were up to something."

Since the apartment was solely in my name, he had nothing to tie him down and was free to leave. I made sure he packed and vacated that same night.

Upon him leaving I thought of how I let him mess up my life with Lisa. I trusted him and vowed that would be the end of our steamy, yet unacceptable relationship.

I immediately called Lisa and apologized for disappearing on her and promised to never do it again if she would take me back.

I was hoping she still loved me, but I had to come clean. I told her about my relationship with Norman and begged for her forgiveness.

Being the good Christian girl, who was about to have my baby any day, she kindly accepted me back, but only if I would marry her. I accepted.

Marriage was going well and out of caution, I had my number changed and deleted the real nemesis.

Norman and I managed to stay away from each other for several months, until one day out of the blue Norman called just to say "hello."

"How did you get my number?" I asked.

"I have my ways." He sexily replied.

"What do you want?"

"I need to see you." He insisted.

"Just tell me what you want. Whatever you need to see me about you can say it over the phone."

"No, I need to see you. Please." He begged.

"Well since we're both married and considering what occurred at the church, where do you want to meet?" I reluctantly asked.

"Please meet me at hotel where we went several months ago. I just want to sit and talk in private. I promise not to make any advances. Just give me one hour."

For some reason I simply had to comply. How I wanted to remind him how much I was hurt by him, but my life was finally where it should be.

I immediately made an excuse to leave as Lisa was preparing dinner. Told her it was an emergency.

I anxiously met Norman outside of the same fleabag hotel he introduced me to. I noticed the same clerk was on duty.

Norman started to talk and apologizing for what he did to me. Then he suddenly inched toward me. I could have inched back, but didn't. For some reason I simply couldn't resist him.

One hour ended up turned into three hours of reminiscent love making. How I missed his touch. He confessed he had paid the desk clerk for three hours in advance, somehow knowing I wouldn't be able to resist his charm.

Again the familiar tap on the room door interrupted our time together.

Time was up.

CHAPTER 18

Upon having arrived home sometime after 2am, I was glad that Lisa was sound asleep. I immediately showered in an attempt to wash the smell of sex off my body. I quietly tried to crawl into bed, when Lisa politely asked,

"So how was your emergency?"

"It's ok now," I pretended to respond in a sleepy tone.

She then began to cuddle next to me in an attempt to have sex. I'm sure she knew something had occurred, particularly since I didn't respond to her ritualistic sexual advances, something we both highly enjoyed. But she never said a word regarding my rejection.

The next morning she got up early and quietly exited allowing me to finish my well-needed rest.

Upon arising, I found a note on the kitchen table which read,

"I'll be at my mom's home for the weekend."

I assumed this was her way of confirming to me without having conflict that she knew I had been unfaithful during my *emergency*.

I immediately called her at her mom's home and said "We need to talk."

"I know," She sweetly responded.

She stayed at her mom's all weekend without calling or coming home for a change of clothes. She apparently had taken some outfits with her.

Upon her arrival late Sunday evening I attempted to go for a hug. But she shrugged her shoulders and scurried away to the living room, sitting politely on the small black leather sofa bed.

"Let's talk." She demanded.

"Lisa, I don't how to explain it but I know you're no way stupid. I must confess. It was Norman that called me last night and wanted to talk. That was my emergency."

"I assumed that much," She responded and continued, "Did you have sex with him?" I couldn't believe she was so direct. But she was and very serious.

"I can't lie, yes." I reluctantly responded. "Will you please forgive me?"

"Yes, but it will take time. I promised God through our wedding vows I would stick by you through thick and thin. I plan to keep my vow and promise to God."

She continued. "But you have to do YOUR part. I don't know what Norman has over you, but whatever it is has to go."

"Please pray with me that God will make me strong enough to resist his and anyone else's advances."

"Yes, gladly," She sweetly responded.

We immediately got on our knees and prayed for not only her forgiveness of me, but also for God's forgiveness and deliverance.

I knew I would be forgiven, but deliverance would be another story. I knew I had to stay strong, not only for our marriage, but also for our baby.

CHAPTER 19

Again, Lisa and I moved and changed our phone number. We knew we had a long hard journey ahead. But we were determined.

A few years passed and not a word from Norman, thank God!!

Her friends became my friends as we began to associate primarily with other married couples.

Life was definitely beginning to take a turn for the better.

One Sunday afternoon we went out to one of her friend's home for a couple's dinner.

The other couple had prepared an awesome meal. Then the ladies said they would clean up and enjoy some girl time talking about what ladies like to discuss.

The other guy and I retreated to the den to watch a game, when he asked me to help him repair a light fixture in the bathroom. He then told the ladies where we were going, so they wouldn't be alarmed to our whereabouts.

It was great finally spending time with another male, doing things men do.

Upon entering the bathroom, he closed the door and climbed up small step-ladder in an attempt to undo the fixture. He then stepped down and faced me.

I noticed he had a slight erection, but I didn't say anything. Suddenly he started to adjust his somewhat erected manhood. The more he adjusted himself the more erect I noticed he became.

Then without shame, he grabbed himself and began to massage his penis to the point of a full erection, and said "Man, we don't have much time, so let me be frank. I'm horny for you and have been for quite some time."

Me being polite because I was at his home replied, "Man, I've never seen you before today. Where do you know me from?"

"At Lisa's church," He responded without hesitation.

Then he continued, "It was in the men's restroom. You were using the urinal next to me. I happened to peep over the partition and saw all that you're working with and immediately got hot.

You must be packing a good nine to ten thick inches."

I proudly stated, "Well, thanks for noticing, and you're in the ballpark." For it's a known fact that most guys like compliments from other guys or like to brag about the size of their genitalia.

"Hey, since the girls are in the other room cleaning up, why don't you *pop it out*. Let me see what you're working with up close and personal? If it's like I remember, you have a pretty dick. I would love to stroke it and give you some quick head."

"I don't do that," I responded. But deep within I began to feel a burning fire in my groin for some adventure. I too was getting horny, since it had been a long time I had the feel of another man's hands or lips on my dick.

Suddenly I became fully erected, which I was trying to hide by placing my hand in my pocket shifting my penis to an upward position, which he obviously noticed.

"Then why are you hard?" He asked.

Who wouldn't get hard at the thought of some good quick head, I thought. Besides, Lisa had never had her lips around my penis. It was something she was adamantly against.

He immediately began to unzip his pants and without further coercion I followed suit. We began stroking each other. Before I knew it, he was down on his knees fulfilling his desire.

I so wanted to tell Lisa what had happened at her friend's home, but kept it to myself. I didn't want to jeopardize our marriage again. Nor did I want Lisa to approach her girlfriend and church member about what her husband and I did. I had to keep that secret.

I obviously had not been *delivered.*

CHAPTER 20

The rest of the week I continued to think about my recent elicit salacious encounter with Lisa's church member. Although it was limited, but rather risqué, thoughts of Norman began to resurface.

Until this short encounter, I was definitely on the verge of no return to a complete heterosexual life.

The brief incident relit the forbidden spark for my love-god, Norman. I had to contact him. Something I promised to not to do.

I managed to contact someone whom I knew had his number and called him one Saturday morning. A call he was eager to take. The excitement in his voice upon hearing me had the resonance as if he had won the lottery. The feeling was mutual.

Luckily, his wife was out of town and Lisa was visiting her sister for the day.

Without hesitation he invited me over for a mid-day rendezvous. I had to go. I had to dance on some hot sand again.

The drive to his place seemed to take too long.

As soon as I entered, we immediately hugged, kissed and fondled each other for at least ten minutes.

He immediately led me up to his bedroom, undressing each other as we climbed the stairs leaving a trail of clothes.

It was there where we completed unveiling each other to complete nudity. Pawing over each other like wild animals. We began to pick up where we left off and somehow finding enough sperm for each of us to have three orgasms with very little rest between sessions.

We now understood the meaning of, "absence making the heart grow fonder."

After hours of seemingly love making like never before, we decided to take a long shower together, something we both sorely missed. We started kissing, hugging and rubbing going for a fourth orgasm, then allowing it to be washed away with the warm soapy water.

It was then I noticed I had left a passion mark on him, which I brought to his attention.

Since he was of dark complexion he said he could easily hide it. Then he pointed out the marks he left on my neck. I began to panic because due to my much lighter complexion, there was no way I could hide it, particularly from Lisa. The hickey stood out like a sore thumb.

Nonetheless, it was there. I somehow had to figure out a way to camouflage it. It was too hot outside for a turtleneck sweater.

When Lisa arrived home, I continued to somehow uncustomarily managed keep my shirt on until bedtime. I made sure all lights were off or at least very dim for several days.

By the third day, it looked like the passion mark was just about gone. I somehow thought she wouldn't see it, so I started to become more relaxed.

As we were having dinner, she surprisingly said. "I see your passion mark is almost gone, so you can stop acting so mechanical."

"What are you talking about?" I questioned, trying to play dumb.

"I saw it two days ago. I just wanted to see how long did you think you could camouflage it without me noticing?" She continued, "I had to turn the light on while you were asleep to look for something and happen to notice it."

I couldn't say anything.

"Who was it? Norman again or do you have a new *boo*?"

"Yes, it was Norman." I responded. Being very embarrassed!

"So other than a penis, what does he have that I don't?"

Again, I've never heard her talk so blunt.

"It's not just the penis." I responded, and continued. "I really can't explain it. I know we prayed over this, but maybe I was just born this way and it took Norman to bring it out."

She quickly responded, "That's not of God and is not His way."

I then came back with "I know where you're going with this, and according to what I've read in the bible, it's not God's. But did you know that King James was allegedly gay?"

"Don't try to twist the words of the bible." She said. "That's blasphemy!"

"I'm not. I'm just telling you what I have heard, read and backed up through deeper research. That research said that King James was gay or at least bisexual.

To my understanding certain passages in the bible were written or interpreted to address the people of THAT day who were promiscuous, which I am not. Believe me, I'm definitely not trying to justify my actions, but I also believe that God doesn't make mistakes. I need to be comfortable in the way He made me."

She sat silent.

I continued, "That's probably one of the reasons why so many youth commit suicide, because they're not accepted for who they really are and trying to follow some archaic ritual of going against their **natural** being."

She continued to sit silent.

"I am so sorry for the hurt I've place on you, but I did try to be faithful." I apologetically stated.

She then broke her silence saying, "If it were another woman I could possibly compete. But it's a man. How do I compete? I can't. I love you." She cried.

"I love you too." I interrupted.

She began to cry, "Then, if you love me, REALLY love me, you wouldn't have done this, particularly with another man. "I need some time away. I'm going to my sister's house for the weekend."

She hastily packed a few items and immediately left.

I walked around our apartment feeling lonely thinking "What have I done and how can I correct the damage?"

It was then another male acquaintance, Carlos, called saying he needed a place for the evening. He said he was going through something and just wanted a place to lay his head for the night and talk.

Since I too needed to talk with someone, although I knew I couldn't express my thoughts in detail, I invited him to come over.

"Sure come on over bro."

Although I hesitated a bit in my response, as I didn't know him very well. Also to my knowledge, he was straight.

All I could think was his timing was great. I was so lonely but also needed someone to talk to. Just talk and vowing to not disclosed to him what was going on in my personal life. Maybe some guy time alone with a male to whom I felt there would be no conflict of interest would help me in my situation.

Carlos was there within the hour.

We ordered pizza and watched TV and laughed until time to retire for the evening without discussing each other's problems.

"Where do I sleep?" He asked.

"Well man, Lisa will be away for the weekend, so if you want, you can sleep on the other side the bed or on the floor."

"If you don't mind, I can sleep on her side of the bed, but no funny stuff." We both laughed.

To my knowledge Carlos was strictly heterosexual, which I welcomed. I assume he never thought nor suspected anything different of me.

In watching him undress, I thought of how nicely cut his Puerto Rican body was, when he abruptly said, "Are you part Puerto Rican or half white?

"Why do you ask?" I responded.

"Well, we're both about the same complexion. In fact, unless my eyes deceive me, you seem to be a tad lighter than me."

We instinctively moved toward each other and compared arms. They were about the same complexion. Then we compared the thighs. He was right. My thighs were a tad lighter.

"You must be part white, then." He jokingly, but comfortable stated.

"Whatever, I'm used to it."

We both chuckled.

As we crawled in bed, I noticed the bulge of his flaccid manhood, as most men would notice about another man and pretend not to admire.

Interestingly, women can and *do* openly comment on each other's perky breasts without thinking less of each other or being ostracized.

I wondered because of his being non-apprehensive about comparing thighs, or was he trying to covertly *make a move* on me, particularly since Lisa was not home.

As it turned out, no *move* was made. Apparently what had gone through my mind were erroneous subliminal erotic thoughts of sharing the same bed with another man other than Norman.

Never once did it occur to me that I had allowed someone else to occupy Lisa's side of the bed. It was complete innocence.

Luckily nothing happened, as I didn't want to compound an already tense situation between me and Lisa, even in her absence.

As Carlos and I slowly awakened having early morning conversation in bed, we heard the locks turn on the front door. It was Lisa who had unexpectedly returned home a day early.

She screamed at the sight of seeing me in bed with another man. I'm sure she must have thought I was having an affair.

She immediately ran out and slammed the door. I tried to catch her to let her know this was simply a friend and nothing sexual was going on.

"It's over." She screamed, as she ran down the stairs and quickly exited the building.

I could hear her sobs and screams as she ran toward her car. Her cries and screams continued as she entered the vehicle and frantically driving away.

Carlos being shocked, "What's going on?" He asked. "It seems you have more problems than me."

"Sorry man." It's all a misunderstanding.

"No problem," he stated, then continued, "Why don't you and your wife iron this out. I definitely don't need no drama or to be a part of something obviously gone awry."

He immediately put his clothes on and left. I never heard from him again.

It seemed as if by not giving her advance notice that Carlos was would be staying with me while she was visiting her sister had done irreparable damage to our failing marriage.

Also, I'm sure at the sight of seeing a man in our bed, regardless of how innocent it was, added to her frustration and hurt.

CHAPTER 21

I immediately attempted to contact her at her sister's home and at work the following week, but she would not take my calls. I wanted so much to explain how it was all a misunderstanding. Then I thought if the *shoe was on the other foot*, as the saying goes, I more than likely would have reacted similarly.

Within one week of a lonely bed and no contact from her, I finally received a letter in the mail from her saying she would be filing for divorce.

I could have tried to talk her out of it, but I understandably knew where she was coming from, so I had to live with the defeat. I had completely messed up.

I had no one to turn to, but Norman.

I had hopes that now the path would be clear for he and I to resume a more stable relationship. I wanted him to leave his wife and move in with me and go for a new start.

I felt deeply within that the rendezvous we recently had was enough to seal the deal. After all it was he who chased and changed me.

To my surprise, he rejected my offer, but said we could still see each other on the **down low**. I was hurt, but reluctantly agreed.

We continued to see each other on a weekly basis, sometimes twice a week which seemed to fill a need.

He often came to my lonely apartment or when his wife was away, he would daringly invite me over for an afternoon tryst.

Deep within knowing how Charlotte now despised me, I was hoping she would have surprised us by showing up early. Then I could hopefully have him to myself.

Unfortunately that never happened, so I eventually came to the realization that I would continually be the *side piece*. I had to open myself to other options.

Although Norman and I continued to see each other, holidays and other special days he was with his loving wife and family. I seemed to continually be alone.

I often thought "How could I so foolishly let him change me? I had an awesome wife." But the damage was done.

Finally after realizing what I had lost with Lisa, I tried without success to get her to take me back. She was always pleasant, but had definitely moved on. She had found herself another man and was pregnant by him.

Fortunately, Lisa and I still remained in contact and I was allowed to call her, primarily because of our child.

One day to my utter amazement I called her and her new husband answered the phone.

"Hey man, how are you?" He asked.

"All is well." I responded. "I hope you don't mind me calling. I was only checking on my baby daughter."

"She's fine." He quickly responded then said, "Lisa and I have been having problems, plus a few other things been going on. I need to get away for little while. I know this may sound out of place, but do you mind if I come and stay with you for a few weeks?"

All I could think of was "What current spouse of someone you were married to would have the nerve to ask an ex-spouse something like that?"

I must say the first thing I thought of was that he was probably, in his own coveted way, trying to make a move on me.

I was so thankful for my newly acquired *gaydar* alert.

I felt it was totally down-right disrespectful. I immediately said, "NO, that wouldn't be right."

That was the last time we spoke. After that I made it a point to only call her on her cell phone or at work.

CHAPTER 22

Although I had numerous opportunities to get with another woman, I soon began to accept my new lifestyle as a gay man. I definitely didn't want to take another female through what I had taken Lisa through. Plus living a dual lifestyle or as more commonly known *on the down low or D.L.* simply was not right.

Holidays were continually becoming very lonely without that special someone in my life. I eventually opened the door to allow other opportunities for male companionship into my life.

After a few dates and sexual encounters, I soon discovered that they were all the same or similar, who had adopted the unsettling sordid mind-frame of the three **F** ideology---*Find 'em, Freak 'em, Forget 'em.*

Others I met were in financial distress and desperately seeking a *Capitan Save-A-Hoe*. Either way, I knew neither was me, nor the way I wanted to live.

Soon I met Jarvis, a tall handsome guy with dark curly hair. He most assuredly didn't seem to capture my sexual interest, but he seemed to be sincere and definitely didn't give the impression of being like the others.

Like Norman, he even introduced me to his mother, who welcomed me into Jarvis' life with open arms.

Although Jarvis' mother was not a church goer, she was very welcoming and spiritual. How I love going to her home to eat after service and even inviting me to spend the night with them.

Jarvis and I got along so well that I soon began to forget about Norman by again moving and having my number changed. I only gave it out to relatives, Lisa and a few select friends.

The start of the new chapter in my life was beginning to feel great. As Jarvis and I continued our relationship, I decided to let him move with me.

One day I had a business engagement and asked Jarvis if wanted to go with me. He said no thanks. That he had something else to do. No problem, as we weren't *tied at the hip*.

I went to my business engagement only to discover I was about three hours too early. I decided to return home.

Upon opening the door, I discovered the unimaginable. Jarvis had obviously contacted someone I thought was a good friend. They were having sex.

"What is this about?" I shouted.

"You weren't supposed to see this. I thought you would be gone for a while. I'm sorry." He pleaded.

"So this is what you do when we're not together?"

He remained silent.

I continued to yell at Jarvis, "And with my pseudo *good* friend. There's no excuse." He knew for sure there would be a fight or confrontation of some sort. I immediately thought about how I lost my temper with Norman at the church.

I quickly gathered my composure, as I didn't want the situation to escalate to something for which I would be sorry.

"You two can continue what you were doing. In fact, you can have each other."

I immediately left in return to my business appointment. Enroute, all I could think about was what had just occurred and my previous experiences with Lisa and Norman. As the saying goes, "What goes around comes around."

Karma is real!

Additional books by **E. McLeod Baines**

Non-Fiction

Secret Doors-Hidden Tales

Secret Doors-Hidden Tales is a chilling memoir of a preteen plagued and tormented by a close family member and how he overcame numerous challenges and negative surroundings to achieve a more successful and productive life.

Non-Fiction

Cookie Power-A Double Standard

Coauthored with Spencer Moon

Cookie Power-A Double Standard is a controversial and very candid and graphic discussion referencing the demographic changes in the workplace and its adverse effect on men, particularly men of color.

Contact Information:

www.ebainesproductions.com

Facebook   Instagram

Made in the
USA
Columbia, SC